P9-CEP-146

FRIENDS
OF ACPL

jE
Falwell, Cathryn.
Christmas for 10

799

HOLIDAY COLLECTION

ALLEN COUNTY PUBLIC LIBRARY
FORT WAYNE, INDIANA 46802

You may return this book to any agency or branch
of the Allen County Public Library

DEMCO

CHRISTMAS FOR 10

by
Cathryn Falwell

Clarion Books/New York

Clarion Books
a Houghton Mifflin Company imprint
215 Park Avenue South, New York, NY 10003
Copyright © 1998 by Cathryn Falwell

Type is 30/33-point Granjon.
The illustrations for this book are collages made from cut paper
and fabric, with watercolor detail.

All rights reserved.

For information about permission to reproduce selections from this book, write to
Permissions, Houghton Mifflin Company,
215 Park Avenue South, New York, NY 10003.

Printed in Singapore.

Library of Congress Cataloging-in-Publication Data
Falwell, Cathryn.
Christmas for 10 / by Cathryn Falwell.
p.   cm.
Summary: Rhyming text presents a traditional Christmas celebration
in which various objects and people are counted.
ISBN 0-395-85581-0
[1. Christmas—Fiction. 2. Counting. 3. Stories in rhyme.]
I. Title.
PZ8.3.F2163Ch   1998
[E]—dc21   97-46134
CIP
AC

Allen County Public Library
900 Webster Street
PO Box 2270
Fort Wayne, IN 46801-2270

TWP 10 9 8 7 6 5 4 3 2 1

For my dad,
Warren David Falwell,
for making Christmas magical

1 one
star
for the top
of the
Christmas
tree

2 two
angels
with wings

3 three
royal
kings

 **4** four
children play
in harmony

 five
snuggle
up near

6 six
stories
to hear

3 1833 03357 2626

7 seven
tasty
candy canes

8 eight
reindeer
that fly

9 nine
ribbons
to tie

**10** ten
hands
string the
popcorn
chains

 one
wreath
welcomes
guests
to the door

2 two
will make

3 three will bake

 four
will taste
and ask
for more

5 five
baskets
to pack

6 six
presents
to stack

7 seven
bright
candles
standing tall

8 eight
voices sing

9 nine
silver bells
ring

10 ten joyful folks wish peace for all!